D0409062

# ABANDONED!
## A Lion Called Kiki

RAINBOW
STREET
SHELTER

# ABANDONED!
## A Lion Called Kiki

by **Wendy Orr**

illustrations by **Patricia Castelao**

Henry Holt and Company ❖ New York

Henry Holt and Company, LLC
*Publishers since 1866*
175 Fifth Avenue
New York, NY 10010
mackids.com

Text copyright © 2012 by Wendy Orr
Illustrations copyright © 2012 by Patricia Castelao

Library of Congress Cataloging-in-Publication Data
Orr, Wendy.
Abandoned! A lion called Kiki / Wendy Orr ;
illustrated by Patricia Castelao. — 1st ed.
p.   cm. — (Rainbow Street Shelter ; no. 4)
Summary: When Mona McNeil returns to visit her grandparents'
farm as an adult, she recalls the summer she spent there raising Kiki,
a lion cub she got as a birthday gift from her uncle Matthew—
an experience that led her to open Rainbow Street Animal Shelter.
[1. Lions as pets—Fiction. 2. Lion—Fiction. 3. Animals—Infancy—Fiction.
4. Grandparents—Fiction.] I. Castelao, Patricia, ill. II. Title.
III. Title: Lion called Kiki.
PZ7.O746Ad 2012   [Fic]—dc23   2011042747

ISBN 978-0-8050-9501-2 (HC)
1  3  5  7  9  10  8  6  4  2

ISBN 978-0-8050-9502-9 (PB)
1  3  5  7  9  10  8  6  4  2

First Edition—2012 / Book designed by April Ward
Printed in the United States of America by
R. R. Donnelley & Sons Company, Harrisonburg, Virginia

For Cappy, and for Jade, who's working
to help lions like Cappy to live free

—W. O.


For Claudia

—P. C.

# 1

For as long as she could remember, Mona had loved animals. Some of her friends loved dogs, some loved cats, and others were crazy about hamsters, but Mona loved all animals.

Her mother said that when Mona was a baby, she'd learned to walk by holding on to her grandparents' dog. The dog was a golden retriever, strong but gentle, and he'd let baby Mona grab his curly blond fur to pull herself up.

Maybe that was why Mona had always known that when she grew up, she was going to work with animals.

But somehow, when she did grow up, she thought that working with animals wasn't a real, grown-up job, and she went to work in an office. Mona worked hard and earned money, but she wasn't happy.

Then, one day, she flew across the country, rented a car, and went back to where her grandparents had lived when she was a little girl.

Rainbow Street was short and narrow. At the very end was an old house with a big yard, shady trees, and a rickety fence. The house looked as if no one had loved it for a long time. The paint was peeling off, and one front window was broken.

It didn't look like the busy, happy home that Mona remembered. She was glad her grandparents couldn't see it now.

Suddenly, a three-legged goat trotted out from behind a tree.

Mona stared in surprise. "Hi there!" she called.

She got her backpack and sleeping bag

out of the rental car and opened the gate. As she watched the three-legged goat nibble its way across the lawn toward her, she felt as if she'd turned back into that little girl who knew exactly what she wanted in her life.

**2**

Twenty-five years earlier, in a cage in a trailer at the back of a circus, a lioness had rustled her straw into a soft bed.

Her sister lioness and the roaring, shaggy-maned lion were performing in the circus big top. Right this minute, the crowd was gasping as they leapt through fiery hoops.

This lioness was resting. She was tired, and her belly was huge. She was getting ready to have cubs.

On the other side of the country, eight-year-old Mona was packing her suitcase to visit her grandparents. For the first time ever, she was going to stay for the whole summer vacation while her mom and dad went to their busy jobs in the city. She was a little bit scared, and very, very excited.

Grammie and Grandpa McNeil lived on the edge of a town near the beach, in a small blue house on Rainbow Street.

"We saw a rainbow the very first time we came here," Grammie explained. "Our house was right under the middle of the arch."

"We knew it would be a place where dreams can come true," said Grandpa.

Mona's dream was that this year, since her birthday was in the first week of the vacation, her parents would let her have a pet of her own.

"You'll have all the pets you want, all summer," her mom said.

"But I want to bring one home," said Mona.

"Our lives are just too busy for a pet," said her dad.

Grammie and Grandpa sometimes said

they were too busy to have any more pets too—but the next time they heard about a stray that needed a home, they always said it could come and live with them till it found somewhere better. Somehow the animals never found anywhere better.

That's why they had five dogs. They had Goldie, the very old retriever who'd taught Mona to walk when she was a baby. Next was Patchy, a spotty little dog who'd just followed Grandpa home one day. Buck was a sort-of border collie, with a white face and a black patch over one eye; he'd turned up in a thunderstorm, and they never found out where he came from. Finally, there were two little wiener dogs, Frieda and Vicky, who'd needed a home

when the old lady who owned them went
to the hospital.

When Mona and her parents had visited
the year before, Grammie and Grandpa
had a brand-new baby goat named Heidi.
Heidi was a twin, but she was smaller and
weaker than her brother, and the mother

goat hadn't had enough milk to feed both of them. "The little one will die if someone doesn't look after it," the goats' owner explained. "But I'm just too busy to give it a bottle every two hours!"

Grammie didn't care about being too busy when there was a baby animal to save. She'd taken the tiny brown and white kid, snuggled it on her lap, and fed it special goat milk from a baby bottle. She'd put old towels in a box in the kitchen and tucked the baby goat into it.

Mona had loved the way Heidi snuggled against her, hungrily sucking her fingers. She'd loved feeding her the bottle, even though the kid sometimes nudged her so hard that the milk spurted all over both of them. And she'd loved taking the tiny goat out to the garden to run and play.

Sometimes in the evenings, if Grandpa fell asleep on the couch, Heidi had climbed on top of him and curled up to sleep on his chest.

But now Heidi was nearly grown up. She lived outside all the time and played tag games with Buck the sort-of border collie. All the McNeils' animals lived happily together, even the ones who could have been enemies.

Back at the circus, while everyone was asleep, four tiny cubs were born in the trailer behind the tents. The mother lioness licked them clean and curled around them in the straw bed. Three of the cubs began to nurse, but the last one born, the tiniest of all, was too sleepy to try.

# 3

Mona's attic bedroom in Grammie and Grandpa's house looked just the way she'd remembered it from last summer. The bedspread was patterned with ducklings, and an old teddy bear that had been her dad's was on the pillow. An envelope was propped up on the bear's scruffy paws.

Inside it were three tickets to the circus and a note:

Happy early birthday!
   These tickets include
a behind- the-scenes tour to
see Amazing, Fearsome, and Cute
Animals with your favorite uncle.
   See you Sunday!
                    Love,
                    Uncle Matthew

Uncle Matthew was Mona's dad's younger brother. Except for their red hair and bright blue eyes, they were as different as two brothers could be. Mona's father worked in an office and was always worried, but Uncle Matthew was a juggler in a circus and never worried about anything.

The circus traveled all over the country. Mona and her parents had seen it in their city the winter before. They'd watched Uncle Matthew juggle small bright balls and long striped batons. And when all the lights in the big top went off, Mona knew that the person in the middle of the ring, tossing flaming torches high into the blackness, was her very own uncle Matthew.

Early on Sunday morning, Mona's mother and father took a taxi back to the airport. Mona wouldn't see them again

until the end of the summer. For a minute, she felt very alone.

Then Grammie's hand, warm and comforting, wrapped around hers. Buck, the sort-of border collie, nosed her a ball to throw, and Grandpa said, "Four more hours till the circus!"

Excitement chased the loneliness right out of her body.

It was the best circus Mona had ever seen. Clowns tumbled, poodles rolled barrels, and Uncle Matthew, juggling silvery rings, danced on tall stilts. The lion trainer cracked his whip, and the lion roared back, his tail swishing angrily. The McNeils'

seats were so close they could see his pink tongue and sharp, pointed teeth.

Mona shivered, held her breath, and clapped till her hands were sore—but she never quite stopped wondering what she was going to see after the show.

Finally, when the rest of the audience was going home, full to the brim with amazement and popcorn, Uncle Matthew tapped Mona on the shoulder.

Mona and her grandparents followed him out of the big top, past the other tents and trailers, to one that smelled of hay and animals.

"Keep very quiet," said the lion trainer as Uncle Matthew led Mona and her grandparents in.

A lioness was lying on the floor of a big cage, with four tiny cubs snuggled against her. She lifted her head and snarled at the strangers. Mona shivered. She didn't need the lion trainer to tell her they shouldn't go any closer.

The cubs were about as big as guinea pigs, with spotty golden brown fur. Their eyes were shut tight; they were blind and helpless, and Mona wanted to hold one more than she'd ever wanted anything in her whole life. She could nearly feel how soft and sweet they'd be to cuddle. It was hard to believe they were going to grow up to be fierce, roaring lions.

But the lioness was glaring, her teeth

and eyes bright in the darkness as she warned them all to keep away from her cubs. All Mona could do was stand outside the cage and think how she would love them if she only had the chance.

# 4

Grown-up Mona knew that the goat in front of her now wasn't Heidi. It was a long time since the McNeils had moved across the country to live closer to Mona and her mom and dad. Heidi had gone with them and had lived to be very old, older than goats are ever supposed to be.

But just for a minute, as she picked a bunch of long grass for the three-legged billy goat, Mona could almost smell spilled milk and love.

At the circus, the morning after the performance, the lion cages were loaded onto trucks. There was no time to waste: they were moving on to the next town and the next show.

In a cage with her mother and sisters, the smallest cub was still sleepy and forgetting to drink. The mother lioness stopped licking her. Even though the mother had never lived in the wild, her instinct told her what to do. All her milk and care was needed for the three healthy cubs so they would survive. She had to abandon the little one.

Grammie invited the girl next door to Mona's birthday lunch. Mona knew they could be friends from the way Sarah said hello to Heidi and the dogs.

She unwrapped the tiny china kitten Sarah had brought her. "Thank you!" she said. "I asked my mom and dad for a real kitten, but they said no."

"So did mine," said Sarah.

"Never mind," said Grammie, shooing the wiener dogs from under her feet as she carried a round pink cake to the table.

"You never know what'll turn up around here!"

The phone rang. The girls giggled as Grammie stayed with her arms up like a conductor, waiting for Grandpa so they could sing "Happy Birthday."

But Grandpa came back looking puzzled. "There's something at the airport for Mona. We've got to pick it up right away."

"Cool!" said Sarah. "I've never been to the airport."

So they sang "Happy Birthday" in the car and then "We're Going to the Zoo," because no one knew a song about going to the airport.

Finally, Grandpa parked outside the freight terminal.

Mona felt fizzy with wondering-what-the-present-could-possibly-be excitement. Her parents had already sent her a Barbie doll in a pink bathing suit, and Grammie and Grandpa had given her the book *Charlotte's Web*, about a runty pig and the spider who saves his life. She had no idea who the mystery parcel could be from or what it could be.

*Maybe Uncle Matthew's forgotten he gave me the circus tickets and has sent me stilts,* she decided. He'd given her juggling balls last year, soft ones filled with seeds, like the ones he used to practice. Stilts wouldn't fit into a mailbox. The parcel must be so long it was getting in people's way.

The more she thought about stilts, the more exciting they seemed. She could learn to dance on them the way Uncle Matthew did, and maybe she'd also join the circus when she grew up.

"I'll let you try too," she told Sarah.

"Try what?" Sarah asked.

"You'll see," Mona said.

"Am I glad to see you!" said the man inside the freight terminal. He disappeared to the back of the building.

Mona felt confused. The terminal was

huge. Stilts couldn't take up that much room!

Her grandparents looked more and more worried.

The man came back with a cardboard box and a cat carrier.

In the carrier, nestled in a blanket, was a tiny lion cub.

# 5

Grown-up Mona sat on the worn front step of the old house and felt memories wash over her. The goat nibbled hopefully at her sandals till she rubbed under his chin, down to his armpits. He nodded happily, just like Heidi used to.

"Would you be scared of a baby lion?" Mona asked him.

The goat burped.

"I didn't think so," said Mona. "Neither was Heidi."

The tiny cub woke up and squawked. Mona knelt in front of the cage as the cub crawled out of the blankets, her milky eyes blinking.

"The poor little thing!" Grammie exclaimed.

Mona opened the door and picked up the cub. The baby animal nuzzled against her, sucking her fingers with its raspy tongue.

"We'll have to get her home and feed her before we can figure out what to do," said Grammie. She took the blanket out of the cage and helped Mona wrap up the cub. "Now she'll feel safe, and you won't get scratched!"

"You'd never scratch me, would you?" Mona whispered to the bundle's furry head. She was sure she could hear a purr of an answer.

"Is it really a lion?" Sarah asked.

"It's really a lion," said Grandpa. He didn't sound happy. "We'd better check the box in case there's a tiger in there!"

But the cardboard box had only three baby bottles, five containers of milk powder, a bag of kitty litter—and an envelope.

Happy birthday, Mona!

I know how much you wanted to hold a lion cub, but I bet you never thought you'd be taking one home for your birthday!

The problem is that the lioness didn't have enough milk for all the cubs. This little girl was the smallest, so she never got enough. The lion trainer was afraid she was going to die because it will be very hard to go on bottle-feeding her and looking after her while we're traveling all over the country. I thought about Grammie raising the little goat last year, and I knew she'd want to help you give this baby lioness the same chance.

Love,
Uncle Matthew

Mona knew her grandparents were annoyed at Uncle Matthew, because they always said that no one should ever give someone else a pet without asking first. But all she could think was *I have my very own lion!*

"Wow," said Sarah. "I've never known anyone who got a lion for their birthday."

"Neither have I!" said Grandpa, and began to laugh. After a moment, Grammie started, and then Sarah and Mona couldn't stop.

"What did you think it was going to be?" Sarah asked.

"Stilts," said Mona, and that started everyone laughing again.

They were still giggling as they got into the car. Mona held the lion cub on her lap.

"What are you going to call her?" Sarah asked.

"Kiki," said Mona. She didn't have to think about it. The name had been waiting there since she was two years old and had played at being a kitty called Kiki.

*And if I name this lion,* she thought, *she'll belong to me*—because she had never wanted anything as badly as she wanted to keep this tiny, helpless cub.

Her grandmother smiled and tickled the little lion under her chin. "Hello, Kiki!"

Sweet as honey, relief rushed through Mona's body. It dissolved the tight worry band around her chest until she felt as floppy and relaxed as the cub drifting off to sleep on her lap.

When they got home to Rainbow Street,

Grandpa shut all the dogs outside, so that nothing would disturb the cub's first feeding in her new home.

Mona didn't want to let go of Kiki for an instant. She carried her into the kitchen and sat cross-legged on the floor. Sarah slid down beside her, gently stroking the cub's velvety head, while Grammie mixed the milk formula.

Grammie poured the formula into a baby bottle and showed the girls how to test the temperature by dripping a few drops onto the insides of their wrists. "If it feels just a little bit warm, it'll be the right temperature for a baby animal," she said.

Kiki was still sound asleep. Mona tickled her mouth with the bottle, but the tiny cub wrinkled her nose and grunted with disgust. Then, when some of the warm milk dripped into her mouth, she finally began to suck.

When the bottle was empty, Grammie lifted Kiki off Mona's lap and rubbed her back till they heard a baby-lion burp.

"That feels better, doesn't it?" Grammie murmured, carrying the cub over to the kitty litter tray and helping her do what baby animals have to do after they've been fed.

Grandpa had already cut the cardboard box down to be a two-week-old-lion-cub bed. Mona folded Kiki's blanket to fit in the bottom and lifted her in. A minute later, the cub was asleep again.

She slept through Sarah's dad coming in to pick Sarah up and exclaiming three times "You've got to be kidding!" when he saw what was in the box.

She slept through everyone singing "Happy Birthday" again while Grammie lit the candles and Mona blew them out, because they suddenly remembered they hadn't ever cut the cake.

She slept through the dogs being allowed in one by one to sniff the box so that they'd know the animal inside was a friend they shouldn't chase.

She slept through Grammie pulling Mona onto her lap and saying, "We'll all do our best for Kiki. But her mother stopped feeding her because she didn't think she could keep her alive, and the lion trainer let Matthew send her to us because he didn't think he could either. It's not going to be easy."

"You kept Heidi alive when no one else could," said Mona.

"And I'll do my best for Kiki," Grammie promised.

"But what's best for Kiki will change as she gets older," Grandpa warned. "And I don't know what your parents are going to say about a lion."

Mona knew that he meant they would say no. But she was sure that once her mom and dad met Kiki, they'd love her as much as Mona did.

# 6

Grown-up Mona watched an old man carry a bag of cabbage and lettuce leaves up the path. The three-legged goat trotted eagerly toward him.

"I see you've met Fred," said the old man. "And I'm Juan. Fred and I are amigos from way back."

Fred butted the bag till Juan handed

him a cabbage leaf. "I've been coming over to see him since the people living here left," he explained. "If I had a house and garden, I'd take him home with me. But I don't think he'd like living in an apartment!"

"Poor Fred," said Mona, though the goat looked very happy with cabbage leaf sticking out of both sides of his mouth. "What happened to his leg?"

"He got out when he was a kid and was hit by a car. It doesn't seem to bother him."

Fred butted the bag again and started munching on a lettuce leaf.

"I'm hoping that whoever lives here next likes goats," Juan added.

"My grandparents loved goats," said

Mona. "This was their home when I was little. They moved away a long time ago, but they loved this house too much to sell it."

"And you loved it too?" asked Juan.

Mona nodded. "I think that's why they decided that when the last people moved out of it, the house would belong to me. Grammie said it was so I could follow my dream. The problem is that I'm not sure what that is."

The first week that she lived with the McNeils, Kiki was sleepy and hungry. She was too weak to complain about being away from the warmth of her mother and sisters, or to notice the new smells and sounds. She needed a bottle every two hours, even at night, because she couldn't drink very much at one time. But soon she started to grow. She drank more and she didn't need her bottle so often. She started crawling faster and farther. Soon she could stand on wobbly legs, and she started being able to see.

The baby bottle was nearly as big as she was, but she liked to lie back in Mona's arms and help hold it between her paws. With her eyes closed dreamily, her tummy got rounder and rounder as the bottle got emptier.

"Greedy guts!" Mona teased, feeling as full of love as Kiki was full of milk.

Sometimes, if they were sitting on the back steps, Heidi would rest her head on Mona's knees, watching as if she remembered being a tiny kid having her own bottle. When the cub was finished and Mona put her down on the grass, the goat nuzzled and licked her.

Mona was glad that Kiki and Heidi were making friends. It was exciting having a lion cub for a pet, but she knew that a grown-up lion might eat a goat. "You wouldn't do that, would you?" she whispered in Kiki's ear. "You're my sweet baby lion! You'd never hurt your friends."

Kiki's raspy tongue licked her face with a promise.

Frieda and Vicky, the wiener dogs, lived mostly inside the house. They sniffed Kiki hello every morning and never snapped if she bumped into them, but when Mona was holding the cub, they whined and poked their heads between her knees, their round brown eyes shining jealously.

Grammie didn't think the dogs would hurt the helpless cub, but she never left them alone together, just in case.

By the time Kiki was four weeks old,

she was nearly as big as the wiener dogs. She could walk on all four legs, wobbling proudly across the floor instead of creeping on her belly. She followed the family around the house, calling them with a scratchy noise that sounded like a frog meowing.

Mona started taking her outside to play on the grass and meet the other dogs. They mostly ignored her, because she wasn't old enough to play, but Heidi always stayed close by her side.

"Heidi thinks she's Kiki's babysitter," Mona told Sarah.

That made Sarah giggle, and Sarah giggling made Mona giggle, and they both laughed so long their stomachs ached.

Because the funniest thing of all was that it was exactly true: the little nanny goat was determined to look after the lion cub.

Sarah came to see Kiki nearly every day. Sometimes she brought her little brother or other friends, and sometimes the friends brought their brothers and sisters and more friends. Finally Grammie had to make a rule that only two kids could come at a time.

"Kiki's still a baby," she explained. "She needs naps!"

Some visitors brought toys for Kiki, cat toys or special lion cub toys they'd made themselves. That was useful, because as

Kiki grew and got stronger, she wanted to play. The more she grew, the more she played—and the stronger she became, the rougher she played. None of her toys lasted for long.

Her teeth were growing, sharp and sore, through her gums. Chewing was the only thing that stopped them hurting, so Kiki chewed. She chewed her rubber bone, and Grammie and Mona rubbed her head and said, "Poor Kiki!"

When Grandpa came in for lunch, Kiki crept under the table and chewed his shoes. Grandpa pushed her gently away and said, "No, Kiki!"

She followed Mona to her bedroom and found the Barbie doll on the bottom shelf

of the bookcase. Kiki grabbed it by its
sticking-out arm and dragged it under the
bed where no one could see. The doll was
even better to chew than the rubber bone
or the leather shoes, because she could
crunch right through the arm.

"Kiki!" Mona called. "Where are you?"

She saw the tip of a golden tail under

her bed and pulled out the lion and the one-armed doll.

"No, Kiki, no!" Mona scolded.

Her lion meowed, round ears twitching, as Mona put the doll on the top of the bookcase.

Mona's anger melted away. She knelt and rubbed noses with the cub. "I love you way more than a Barbie doll," she whispered.

Grammie had looked after lots of baby animals, but never a lion. She didn't know whether she should be feeding Kiki meat as well as milk, or what else they should be doing to look after her.

"Why don't we ask the zoo?" said Grandpa.

"NO!" shouted Mona. "They might want to take her!"

"We have to find out what's best for Kiki," said Grammie. "No matter what happens."

So they went to see a veterinarian at the city zoo. She gave them the milk formula that Kiki needed and said that the cub wouldn't be ready to start eating meat till she was about ten weeks old. She said to call right away if Kiki ever got sick.

But she also said that lions couldn't live with people forever.

"Because they're not just big kitties— they're wild animals," Grammie reminded

Mona that night, as the cub snuggled into the girl's lap with her bedtime bottle.

"Kiki's different!" Mona protested, burying her face in her friend's soft fur. "She'd never be wild!"

Grammie stroked Mona's dark hair and didn't answer.

# 7

"There's something very special about loving a four-legged friend," said Juan, sitting down beside Mona to feed the goat the rest of the cabbage and lettuce leaves.

The goat rubbed his nose against the old man's hand.

"Sorry, Fred," said Juan. "Of course, three-legged friends are the best of all."

Mona laughed.

"I'd be happy to come and help look after him, if you move in," Juan added.

"I think Fred would like that," said Mona.

Suddenly, she felt a tiny seed of an idea start to grow at the back of her mind. It was so small she wasn't sure exactly what it was, but she knew that if she waited, it would sprout into something good.

Kiki kept on growing. Her milky-blue eyes were turning golden brown. By the time she was six weeks old, she was as big as a grown-up house cat.

But she was still a baby. She slept all

night in her box in the kitchen. When Mona picked the cub up in the morning, she was always sound asleep, warm and floppy.

"Hello, sleepyhead," Mona teased, rubbing her face against the lion's. She carried her out to the litter tray in the garden. The cub squatted to do what she was supposed to, then stumbled back so sleepily that Mona laughed and picked her up again.

"Are you awake enough for breakfast?" Mona asked. She settled herself into a chair with the cub on her lap as her grandmother handed her a warm baby bottle.

Kiki smelled the milk and squawked excitedly. Her voice still sounded more like a frog than a lion. She grabbed for the bottle with both paws, patting it happily as she sucked. It didn't take long to feed her now.

Buck, the sort-of border collie, taught her to play wild tag and wrestling games. Kiki liked that even more than ball games with Mona, because Buck let her climb all over him and somersault off his back.

Heidi played tag with them too, but she sometimes had to butt the dog and lion to remind them that she didn't like wrestling.

Uncle Matthew called when Kiki was nearly seven weeks old. "How's the cub?" he asked.

"She's beautiful!" exclaimed Mona.

"Are you training her?" he asked.

"She always comes when she's called," Mona said proudly.

"She'll be the best-trained circus lioness ever!" said Uncle Matthew.

Mona felt as if she'd fallen into a pit of ice. She thought maybe her ears were frozen, because it took a long time for her to hear the words and understand them.

But when she did, the ice turned to fire.

"Kiki is *never* going to be a circus lion!" Mona slammed the phone down hard, hanging up on her favorite uncle. She remembered Kiki's father sitting on his stool, roaring at the lion trainer, and she felt that roar inside her, a red rage bursting to get out.

Instead she scooped the cub into her arms, holding her as tight as she could.

But Kiki wasn't in a cuddling mood; she'd been playing tag with Buck, and she wanted to get back into the game. She rubbed her nose politely against Mona's face and then scrabbled to get down. Her back claws scratched Mona's left arm as she jumped.

It was a big scratch, and it bled a lot.

The pain muddled into the pool of anger, sadness, and fear until Mona couldn't hold it any longer. She burst out howling.

Her grandmother came running. Her face turned white when she saw the blood on Mona's arm and T-shirt.

"She didn't mean to!" Mona hiccupped, trying to wipe her tears away and smearing blood all over her face.

"I know. The problem is that she's a lion and doesn't know how strong she is." Grammie cleaned the scratch with purple lotion before covering it with a bandage. "What did Uncle Matthew have to say?"

"He wants Kiki to go back to the circus when she's big."

"No way," Grammie said simply.

Mona felt as if an elephant had been lifted off her shoulders.

"But he's not completely wrong," said Grammie. "You know you can't take her home with you. And even if your parents changed their minds about a pet, Kiki's just shown why she can't live with you forever."

# 8

"So did the cub go back to the circus?" Juan asked. His face was tense, as if he was living the story.

"No," said Mona. "I love my uncle, and I love the circus—the acrobats and jugglers and all that excitement. But it's not the right place for wild animals, and especially not Kiki. She was used to running around the garden and playing. She loved splashing in her wading pool and was very good at climbing trees. In fact, she made sure I got good at it too!"

"I didn't know lions climbed trees." said Juan.

"Some do," said Mona. She pointed to the big trees along the back fence. "Those trees were smaller then, but they were tall climbing trees for a nine-year-old girl and a lion cub."

Grandpa made Kiki a scratching post when she was a few weeks old so she could practice sharpening her claws on that instead of the couch. He covered it with a scrap of carpet, because that's how cats like their scratching posts.

But Kiki was not a cat, and her teeth needed to grow bigger and stronger than any kitty's. She chewed and scratched the post when she had nothing more exciting to do, but most of the time she liked real wood better. A few days after Uncle Matthew called, she chewed chunks out of one leg of the kitchen table. Grammie thought it was funny. She knew she'd like telling people that the table had been carved by a lion.

But that's not what she told Kiki. "Naughty lion!" said Grammie. "Go outside till you can be good!"

Kiki stalked out to the garden and started scratching the bark of a big magnolia tree. The feel of its bark under her claws was even better than the table leg.

Suddenly she saw a squirrel in the branches above her. Kiki was much too

young to hunt, even if she'd had a mother lion to teach her, but she knew that she wanted to chase the squirrel.

She pulled herself up onto a low branch.

The squirrel chattered at her.

The lion cub scratched and climbed higher. The squirrel chattered again, and Kiki climbed to a higher branch.

The squirrel disappeared into the top of the tree. Kiki pulled herself up onto the next branch.

Grammie had told Mona to wait before she followed Kiki out to the garden, because she wanted the cub to remember that she'd been naughty. It felt like a long three minutes before Mona could grab a ball and go out to play with her.

"Kiki!" she called, waiting for her friend to come rushing, bumping and rubbing her head against Mona's knees with happy lion grunts.

Frieda and Vicky looked up from their afternoon naps in the sunny living room. Freckles and Buck came running from different snoozing spots in the garden, in case Mona was going to feed Kiki something delicious. Only Goldie, too deaf to hear, went on sleeping.

But Kiki was nowhere to be seen.

"KIKI!" Mona shouted.

A growly meow came from the magnolia tree. Mona had never heard the cub make exactly that noise before, but she knew it was a frightened noise. She looked up and saw Kiki lying on a high branch, with her legs dangling on either side.

Mona raced to the bottom of the tree. "How did you get up there?"

"Meow!" said Kiki.

Mona was pretty sure that meow meant "It doesn't matter how I got up here—just get me down!"

Mona started to climb. The magnolia tree was her favorite climbing tree, but she'd never gone as high as the branch where Kiki was now. It didn't look strong enough to hold her.

She scrambled up to the branch below and caught her breath. Holding the trunk with one arm, she reached toward the

cub. She could almost touch her—nearly, nearly . . . but not quite. "Come on, Kiki," Mona coaxed. "Just wiggle backward. I'll help you."

"Mona!" Grammie called. "Can't you find Kiki?"

"Up here!" Mona shouted. "I can't quite reach—"

The lion cub wriggled away from her hand, farther down the branch.

"Kiki, stop!" Mona shouted, but now the thin end of the branch was sagging under the cub's weight. Kiki couldn't stop, she was slipping and sliding . . . and before Mona could say anything more, the cub was springing right off the thin, whippy end of the branch.

Straight over the back fence into the Hoovers' yard.

Mona slipped down the trunk as fast as she could, tearing her bandage and skinning her hands and knees.

"Are you all right?" her grandmother called.

"Kiki's in the Hoovers' backyard!" Mona panted, sucking the blood off her hand.

Grammie sprinted to the fence. The fence was tall, and Grammie wasn't, but she pulled herself up and over like an acrobat in Uncle Matthew's circus. By the time Mona scrambled over behind her, her grandmother had already run right through the garden to the road on the other side.

The Hoovers were nice people and good neighbors. They didn't have any pets, but they probably wouldn't mind a lion cub in their yard just this once.

The problem was that because they didn't have any pets, the Hoovers didn't have a fence across the front of their garden. Kiki could run straight out of their backyard and down the street. And frightened animals can run a long way.

"Did you find her?" Juan asked anxiously.

Mona nodded. "She got such a fright that she hid in the first place she saw. Luckily, that was under a hydrangea bush by the Hoovers' back step. She was very happy to have my grandmother carry her home."

"Poor little thing!"

Mona had told people this story before. Most people laughed when she described the little lion flying off the branch into the next-door garden. That was why she didn't tell most people about it anymore.

Because what she remembered was the way it seemed to happen in slow motion, as if she ought to have been able to stop it. She remembered the way her chest felt almost too tight to breathe.

And she'd never forget spotting the tawny lion cub under the big blue flowers. It sounded like a birthday-card cute picture, but it wasn't, because Kiki was

too afraid to recognize her at first. For those few moments, the cub was a wild animal, with her eyes wide and her ears flattened back. In her terror, she could have scratched or bitten without knowing what she was doing.

Mona remembered lying quietly on the ground in front of the bush, murmuring the things Kiki liked to hear. Finally the cub's breathing had settled, her eyes had calmed, and she'd let Mona pat her. Then she crawled out to be rescued and turned into a pet again.

When Mona's grandfather had come home from work, he cut off every branch in the yard that dangled over a neighbor's fence.

"I hate thinking of an animal being so frightened," said Juan, scratching the goat under his whiskery chin. "That's why I've decided that now I've retired and can do what I like, I want to work with animals who need help."

"Like Fred?" asked Mona.

The old man laughed as the three-legged goat rubbed his head up and down Juan's leg. "Like Fred," he agreed. "But there's only one Fred. I figure I should be able to help more animals than that."

"That's what I've always wanted to do too," said Mona. "But what I know about is working in an office."

"I bet you know more than you think," said Juan.

The idea seed at the back of Mona's mind sprouted a shiny new leaf.

# 9

Uncle Matthew called again.

"Kiki's not going to be in the circus!" Mona said.

"None of the cubs are," said her uncle. "The lion trainer's going to retire when these lions are too old to perform. Kiki's sisters are going to a zoo."

"A zoo!" Mona exclaimed.

"The lion enclosure is fantastic. They'll love it!"

"Maybe," said Mona.

"You should send Kiki there too," said Uncle Matthew. "She'd be better off living with other lions instead of people and dogs—and goats."

"Kiki loves us!" Mona shouted. "She's not going to the zoo!"

She said good-bye quickly, before Uncle Matthew could say anything else.

The cub was watching her anxiously. She didn't like Mona to shout.

"Sorry, Kiki," said Mona, rubbing behind the golden ears.

Kiki purred and rolled onto her back to have her tummy rubbed, gazing up at her girl through dreamy half-closed eyes. A wriggly worm of happiness twisted inside Mona, swallowing the hard nut of fear. She thought she would never love anything as much as she did this little lion.

Even though there were no other lions for Kiki to copy, the more she grew, the more she loved chasing and pouncing games, as if she was learning to hunt. She jumped on the vacuum cleaner when Grammie was cleaning. She dragged huge bones around the house and garden, guarding them from the dogs. She chased balls with anyone who'd throw or kick one for her.

Her favorite game was grabbing Goldie's

tail with her front paws and walking around behind him on her hind legs. When the golden retriever was bored with the game, he just sat down on her. When he got up again, Kiki always left him alone for a while.

Her second favorite game was jumping out at Mona and her grandparents from behind the sofa. Once she leapt on Mona's back so hard that she knocked the girl down. No one else saw, and Mona didn't tell.

Now Kiki was in the backyard stalking Sarah's little brother. He was one of her favorite people to play with. He was waiting at the bottom of the back steps, and Kiki knew he hadn't seen her, because he was staring at the door. She crept silently through the flower bed, flattening marigolds and petunias—and with a mighty leap, pounced on his back.

Sarah's little brother crashed facedown onto the steps.

His chin gushed blood. He screamed so loudly that Kiki fled to the fattest hiding bush at the farthest end of the yard.

She stayed there while Mona, Sarah, and Grammie came running. She stayed there while Sarah's mom ran from next door and carried the little boy to the car. When Mona came to coax her out, Kiki purred and rubbed against her to say sorry.

But when Sarah's little brother got home from the emergency room with two stitches in his chin, their mom said that he and Sarah weren't allowed to go over to the McNeils' house anymore.

Suddenly Mona couldn't pretend any longer that her mother and father would let her take a lion home. It was like wishing she could grow wings and fly. It was impossible.

"Can Kiki stay with you when I go home?" she asked her grandmother.

"I wish she could," Grammie said, hugging Mona. "I wish she could stay little and cute and happy living here like a kitty-cat. I wish you could stay here forever too! But life doesn't work like that. Kiki will get bigger, and you'll go back to your parents."

"But I'll come to visit! She'd still remember me!"

"It's not just about whether we can go on living with Kiki. Matthew's right that staying with us isn't fair to her. She's a lion, not a pretend dog or goat. We all need to find out what we should do in our lives: Kiki's job is to find out how to be a lion."

Mona buried her head under her pillow. She didn't want to hear any more.

That night Mona dreamed of a land with golden hills rolling down to a wide blue lake. Zebras and antelope grazed, giraffes nibbled tall branches, hippopotamuses splashed in the water, and elephants trumpeted.

But most of all, there were lions. Magnificent, roaring, king-of-the-beast lions dozed under trees, sleek lionesses stalked through long grass, and playful cubs wrestled over logs. Mona was in the middle of them, rolling, growling,

and chasing with the tumble of young lions.

She looked down at her paws and realized she was a lion too. She was Kiki, wild and free, in a place where she belonged.

Mona woke up feeling happy and didn't know why. Nothing had changed since she'd cried under her pillow in the dark.

But when she went out to the kitchen and bent to greet her sleeping cub, she remembered her dream.

"You were in Africa, Kiki!" she whispered.

The cub's ears twitched as Mona told her about the hills, the animals, and the blue water hole. She seemed to like it so much that when Grammie came in, Mona told her about the dream too.

"We should find out how she can do it," said Grammie.

Mona wondered if her grandmother had gone crazy. "It was just a dream!"

"Sometimes we have to follow our dreams," said Grammie.

# 10

Mona's dream was to send Kiki back to Africa, because that's where lions come from. Grammie and Grandpa helped her call or write letters to people who would know how to help.

Everyone told them the same thing: they couldn't send Kiki straight to Africa.

Instead, what they could do was to take her to a safari park, where she could be safe and almost free.

The best safari park was nearly halfway between Rainbow Street and the city where Mona lived with her parents.

So Mona wrote a letter.

Dear President of the Safari Park,

I have a lion cub named Kiki. She is very smart and loving. She's well behaved, but she needs to live with other lions. I would like her to go to Africa so she could be free, but if she can't, I hope she can go to live in your park.

*I know that everyone in your park would love her.*

*Yours sincerely,*
*Mona McNeil*

Writing that letter was the hardest thing Mona had ever done.

Four days later, a letter arrived in the mail with a brochure showing wide hills and trees, lions dozing and giraffes grazing. The letter said

**Dear Mona,**

**The only way that Kiki could go to Africa is if we had several other female**

cubs her age. If they could form their own pride, we could send them all to a wildlife sanctuary in Zambia. There, they could learn how to hunt and live in the wild, and eventually be completely free.

Unfortunately, we don't have any female cubs roughly the same age as Kiki.

However, we're very excited to have her come and live with us. We believe she will be safe and happy, and we know we will love her.

Yours sincerely,
Kathy Harris
Safari Park Manager

"It does look like a beautiful place," Grammie said, studying the brochure.

"She'll be well looked after," said Grandpa.

The lump in Mona's throat was too big for her to answer. She knew this was the best place for Kiki to go. She just wished she'd never dreamed of something even better.

A week later, they started out on the long journey to take Kiki to her new home, and Mona back to her old one.

Kiki was twelve weeks old. She was about as big as a medium-sized dog and loved riding in the car. Mona laughed out loud at the surprised looks on people's faces as they drove past and saw a lion staring out the window.

Late that afternoon, they pitched their tent in a campground that allowed pets if they were on leashes. The sign didn't say if lions counted as pets.

Mona clipped a leash onto Kiki's collar. She wanted the cub to run with her, but the more she tugged, the harder Kiki tugged back and growled. "I'm not a happy dog—I'm an unhappy lion!" her flattened ears seemed to say.

"Sorry, Kiki," Mona said sadly.

She got a ball out of the car. Kiki's ears twitched forward again. It was her favorite blue ball. Grandpa changed the leash for such a long rope that Kiki couldn't feel it pulling on her collar, and Mona and her lion played a crazy ball game in a circle around him.

That night Mona lay awake as long as she could. She wanted to burn every minute with Kiki into her memory so that

it would be there forever. As she snuggled
her sleeping bag around the lion cub's bed,
Kiki grunted lovingly and fell asleep
sucking Mona's thumb.

They left early in the morning before
the campground was awake. Not even the
sun was up. Mona and Kiki curled up and
let the car rock them back to sleep.

When Mona woke up again, they were parked in front of tall gates. WILDLIFE SAFARI PARK, said the sign.

Grandpa was talking to a man at the gate, and a smiling woman in a khaki uniform was coming toward them.

"Welcome, Kiki!" said the woman. "I'm Kathy!"

Mona's hands were shaking, and her insides felt as if they were being ripped in two. "I've changed my mind!" she wanted to shout. "I can't leave her here all alone!" She didn't say it. Even if she could talk her parents into moving next door to the safari park, it wouldn't be fair to Kiki. The cub wouldn't know if she was a wild animal or a pet.

But she didn't want Kiki to see her cry. She wiped away the hot tears leaking from her eyes and got out of the car with her lion.

"I've got good news for you," Kathy smiled, bending down to rub behind the cub's ears. "The city zoo has just been given three lioness cubs from a circus. They've agreed to send them here to form a pride with Kiki."

"I bet those cubs are her sisters!" Mona exclaimed. "Kiki, you're going to see your sisters again!"

"Perfect!" said Kathy. "Because if they are together, they've all got a chance to be set free."

"In Africa?" Mona asked.

"Yes, the sanctuary in Zambia. It has a wonderful program of teaching cubs born in zoos how to be wild again. Kiki's a lucky little lioness: she'll be safe, but completely free, where she belongs."

Mona nodded. Tears were leaking out faster than she could stop them now. She couldn't speak; her chest was squeezing so tight she could hardly breathe. She hadn't known that anything could hurt this much.

"Meow?" Kiki squawked, and stood up on her hind legs to wrap her front paws tightly around her girl. Mona hugged her back, hiding her face against the cub's neck as her tears soaked into the golden fur.

"Good-bye," Mona whispered.

More than twenty years later, telling the
story still brought tears to Mona's eyes.

"After I got home, the safari park sent
me a picture of Kiki playing with her

sisters. Later I got photographs from the wildlife sanctuary in Zambia, when the cubs were learning all the things their mother would have taught them if they'd been born wild."

"Was that the last time you heard of her?" Juan asked.

Mona smiled. "No. A few years later, the wardens sent me another photograph, of Kiki with two cubs. My little lion, born in a circus trailer, was living her natural life and raising her cubs wild and free. My dream for her had come true."

"Then isn't it time you did what your grandmother told you," asked the old man, "and follow your dreams for yourself?"

Mona thought about it all night. By the time the full moon was fading into the pale gray sky, she knew what she had to do.

Nearly everyone she knew was going to say it was a crazy idea. But the longer she thought about it, the more excitement tingled through her. Mona wanted to feel like that all the time.

"Okay, Grammie," she said to the empty room, as the first rays of the morning sun streamed in the window. "I'll do it."

She rolled over and finally went to sleep. When she woke up, she went straight to the beach and walked for miles along the hard-packed sand at the water's edge. Two hours later, the idea still felt as bright and glistening as the sunlit waves rolling in at her feet.

The next day, Mona went back to the city where she'd lived for so long. She quit her job and packed up her apartment. Then she flew back across the country to start making her new life.

She found an apartment not far from Rainbow Street.

And then she went to an old building in the middle of town. The sign in front said CITY ANIMAL SHELTER. Mona took a deep breath and opened the front door.

She walked past the kennels and cages. There were big dogs, small dogs,

curly-haired dogs, smooth spotty dogs; there were white, gold, brown, and black dogs. There were delicate kitties and fluffy cats. There were lop-eared bunnies and floppy-haired guinea pigs.

Mona tried not to look, but she couldn't help seeing. Now that she knew exactly what her dream was, she didn't know what she was going to do if she couldn't make it come true.

She took the elevator up to the offices on the top floor.

Her hands were shaking as she knocked. She'd been to lots of business meetings before. She'd just never been to one that could change her life.

A secretary with polished fingernails showed her into an office where a man and two women in suits were sitting on the other side of a long table. Mona sat down across from them.

"I want to turn my grandparents' house into an animal shelter," Mona explained. "And I want the job of running it."

"There needs to be more than one person to run an animal shelter," said one of the women.

"I've already got one volunteer," said Mona.

The people in suits looked at each other. "We do need another shelter," the other woman said at last. "There isn't enough room here for all the animals that need help."

"There'll be a lot of things to work out," the man warned.

"It's not like having your own pets at home," the first woman explained. "You'll start to love some of the animals, but you have to give them up when they find the right home."

"I learned how to do that a long time ago," said Mona.

# 11

The City Animal Shelter sent painters
and carpenters to help Mona turn her
grandparents' house into a proper animal
shelter. The reception area had chairs for
people who were waiting, and a big desk
where Mona would meet the animals that
came in. On the wall she hung a framed
photograph of Kiki and her cubs.

"Because it was Kiki who showed me my dream," Mona told Juan.

Across the hall was the examination room, where the visiting veterinarian would check the animals, and the surgery where the sick ones would be treated. There were rooms with cages for small animals like guinea pigs and gerbils.

Outside the back door was a big aviary for birds and an enclosure with trees and hollow logs for wild animals that needed to be looked after before they could be set free again.

"At least they won't have to go all the way to Africa!" said Mona.

There were cat and rabbit areas, separated by wooden walls so the cats and bunnies didn't have to see each other, and neither of them had to see the dogs.

The dog enclosure was the biggest. The kennels were in a U around a lawn with two shade trees and a few bushes. Each kennel had its own run, but Mona planned for the dogs to take turns playing in the center lawn.

There was a tall new wire fence around the whole garden and a water trough for Fred and any other goats who might come to stay.

Everything was clean and fresh. The house was pale blue, just like it had been when Mona was a child, but the door was a cheery, cherry red. Over the door, she'd painted a bright, seven-color rainbow.

The grand opening of the Rainbow Street Animal Shelter should have been a bright and beautiful day. It should have had sunshine, blue skies, and singing birds.

Instead, rain tumbled down, thunder thundered, and lightning flashed in the black sky.

"Maybe it'll stop by the time they all get here," Juan said hopefully.

Everyone was coming at ten o'clock: the mayor, the people in suits from the City Animal Shelter, photographers, reporters, and best of all, lots of people who cared about animals.

The rain didn't stop.

Juan tied a ribbon across the front gate.

A newspaper reporter drove up. He got

out of his car and stepped into a puddle. There were no crowds of people to take pictures of, just a young woman, an old man, and a three-legged goat huddled under an umbrella. The reporter got back into his car and drove away.

The mayor and the man and two women in suits from the city shelter arrived a minute later. The mayor looked around for the reporters and, when he couldn't see any, snipped the soggy ribbon anyway. They all raced down the path to the front door.

"Congratulations," the mayor said, shaking hands with Mona and Juan.

Mona showed them around the building. The city shelter people looked out the windows at the outside enclosures and said how wonderful everything looked. They thanked her for donating the building and said they looked forward to working with her.

Then they scurried back through the raindrops to their cars. Mona and Juan stood at the gate to watch them drive away.

Mona sighed. It wasn't quite how she'd imagined the first day of her dream.

"Look!" said Juan.

A bedraggled gray parrot was flapping wearily toward them. Flying low over their heads, it landed in the tree near the red front door. It looked wet, miserable, and lost.

"Hola, amigo," Juan called softly.

The bird cocked its head warily.

"He's scared," Mona murmured. "I'm afraid he'll fly away if we get too close."

"He's hungry," Juan said. "Hold on, amigo. You've come to the right place for a treat!"

Mona waited at the gate as the old man walked slowly around the garden to the back of the house. Wherever the bird had come from, it needed help now. She watched in case it tried to fly away before Juan came back.

"You look like you've traveled a long way," she told it. "We should call you Gulliver—at least till you find your own home!"

Suddenly she realized that the rain had stopped. The sun came out, and for a moment she stood blinking in the brightness.

When she could see again, Juan was standing in front of the little blue house with the gray parrot eating birdseed from his hand.

Above them was a rainbow.

# COMING SOON:

Come to Rainbow Street Shelter
and meet your **new best friend!**

Some of the pets are lost.

Some of them have never had a home.

But all of them need **someone to love**.